What do sled dogs do when they can no longer pull a sled? Follow Black Bear on her journey of discovery in the Black Bear Sled Dog book series.

Dedicated to some of the retired sled dogs who have taught me so much: Black Bear, Copper, Comet, Swannie, Lefty, Chabo, Twosome, Gazelle, Hippo, and Brush.

This book series helps support retired Alaskan sled dogs.
www.blackbearsleddog.com

First Edition

ISBN 978-1-7322303-6-1

Library of Congress Control Number: 2020931842
Printed in the United States of America

Published by Brown & Lowe Books
Springfield, VA
www.brownlowebooks.com

Life Lessons from a Sled Dog

Featuring Black Bear Sled Dog and Friends

Written and Illustrated by
Denise Lawson

From sled dogs who traveled
thousands of miles,

Some simple life lessons
to spread lots of smiles.

Explore with friends,
and get outside.

Take plenty of time
to enjoy the ride!

Every day is a good day to run.

A snow angel at any age
is sure to be fun!

Pull your weight,
and do your best.

Go to bed early,
and get plenty of rest.

Be thankful
for the food you eat.

Take good care
of your hard-working feet!

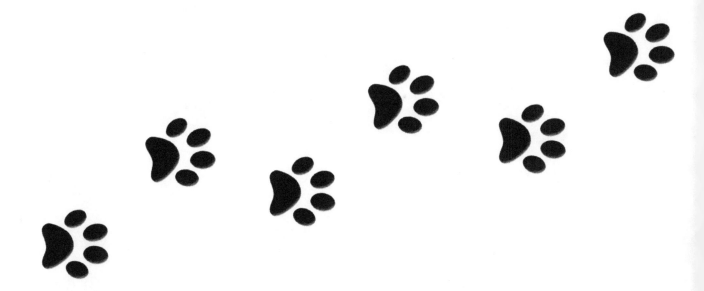

Be ready to lend
a helping hand,

Ask questions
when you don't understand.

On days when you just
aren't sure what to do,

Find a way
to celebrate you!

CPSIA information can be obtained
at www.ICGtesting.com
Printed in the USA
JSHW041527200123
36428JS00002B/10